My Very First Look at

Shapes

TWO-CAN™
PRINCETON ■ LONDON

Published in the United States and Canada by
Two-Can Publishing LLC
234 Nassau Street
Princeton, NJ 08542

For information on Two-Can books and multimedia,
call 1-609-921-6700, fax 1-609-921-3349, or visit our website at
http://www.two-canpublishing.com

Conceived, designed and edited by

Picthall & Gunzi Ltd

21A Widmore Road, Bromley, Kent BR1 1RW, U.K.

Original concept: Chez Picthall
Editor: Lauren Robertson
Designer: Dominic Zwemmer
Photography: Steve Gorton
Additional photographs: Daniel Pangbourne
DTP: Tony Cutting, Ray Bryant
Cover design: Paul Calver

Two-Can Publishing is a division of Zenith Entertainment Ltd,
43–45 Dorset Street, London W1U 7NA

HC ISBN 1-58728-238-0
SC ISBN 1-58728-278-X

HC 1 2 3 4 5 6 7 8 9 10 03 02 01
SC 1 2 3 4 5 6 7 8 9 10 03 02 01

Printed in Italy by Eurolitho

My Very First Look at
Shapes

Christiane Gunzi

PRINCETON ■ LONDON

Circles

ping pong ball

yo-yo

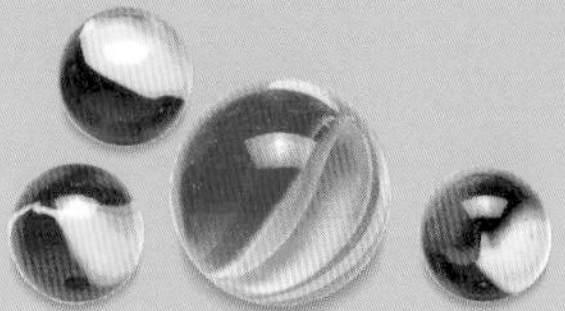

marbles

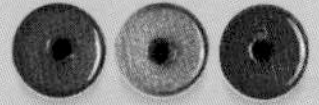

beads

cake

beach ball

ball of yarn

What color is the yo-yo?

orange

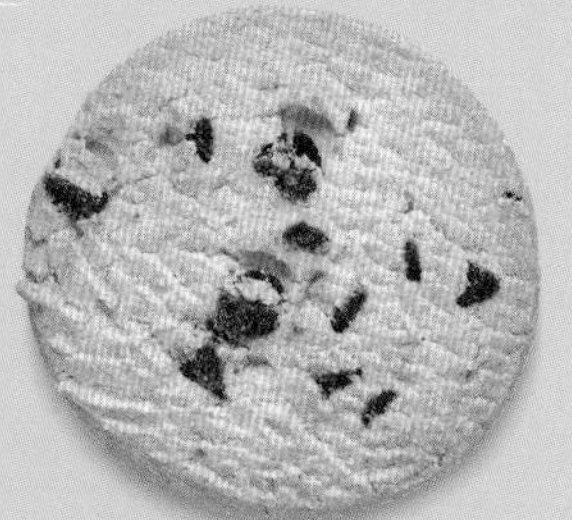
cookie

tennis ball

coins

clock

buttons

paperweight

daisy

How many balls can you see?

Triangles

flags

coat hanger

cookies

sandwich

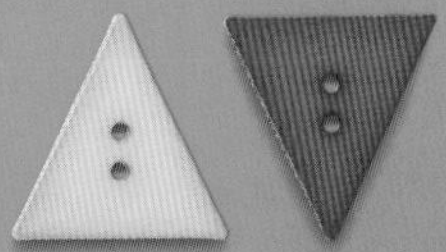

buttons

How many flags do you see?

cheese

cake

fan

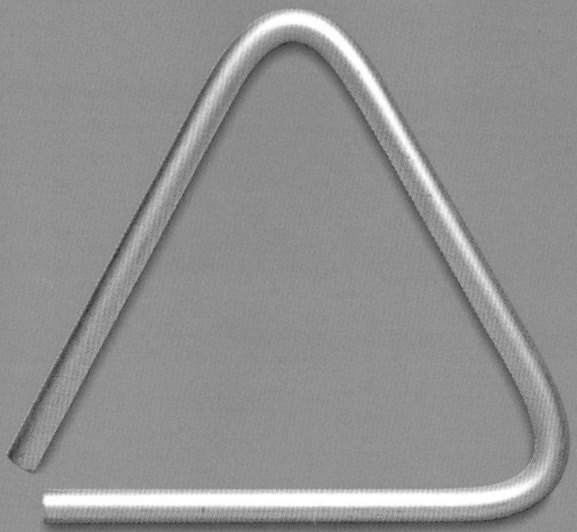

triangle

party hat

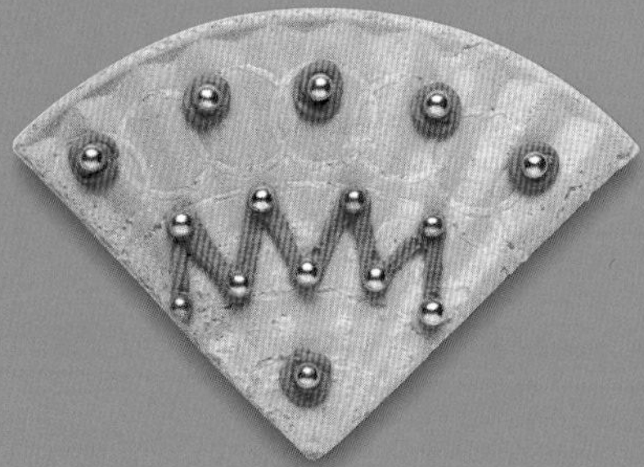

cookie

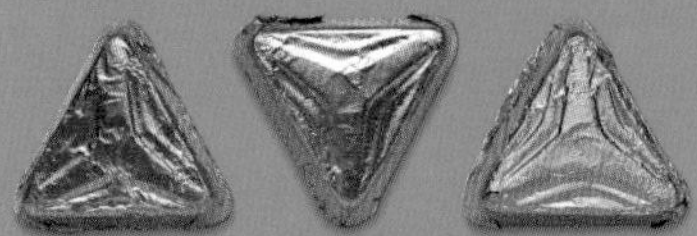

chocolates

Is there anything you can wear?

Squares

box

book

tile

pictures

jack-in-the-box

What can you see on the tile?

present

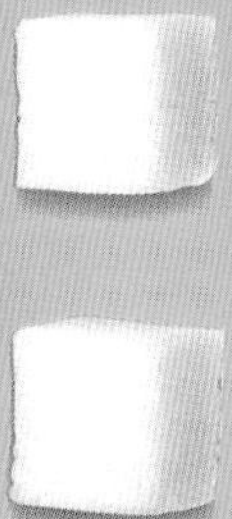

sugar cubes

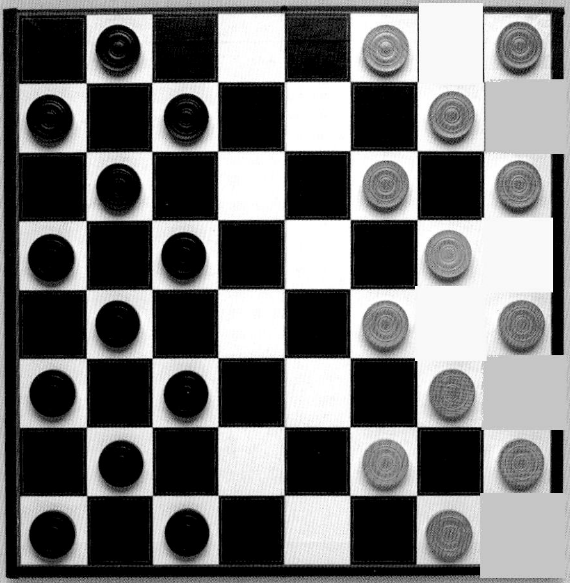

game

candy

blocks

handkerchief

cake

How many cakes can you count?

Rectangles

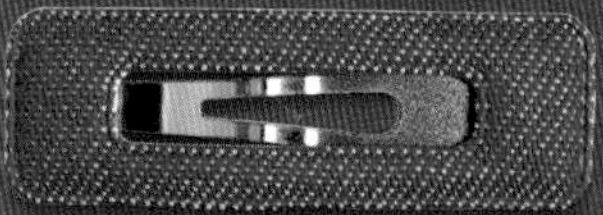

barrette

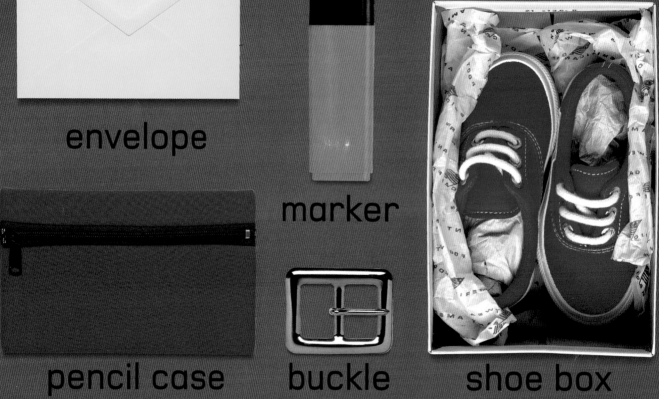

envelope

marker

pencil case

buckle

shoe box

Can you see something silver?

box of paints

chocolate

book

comb

ruler

clay

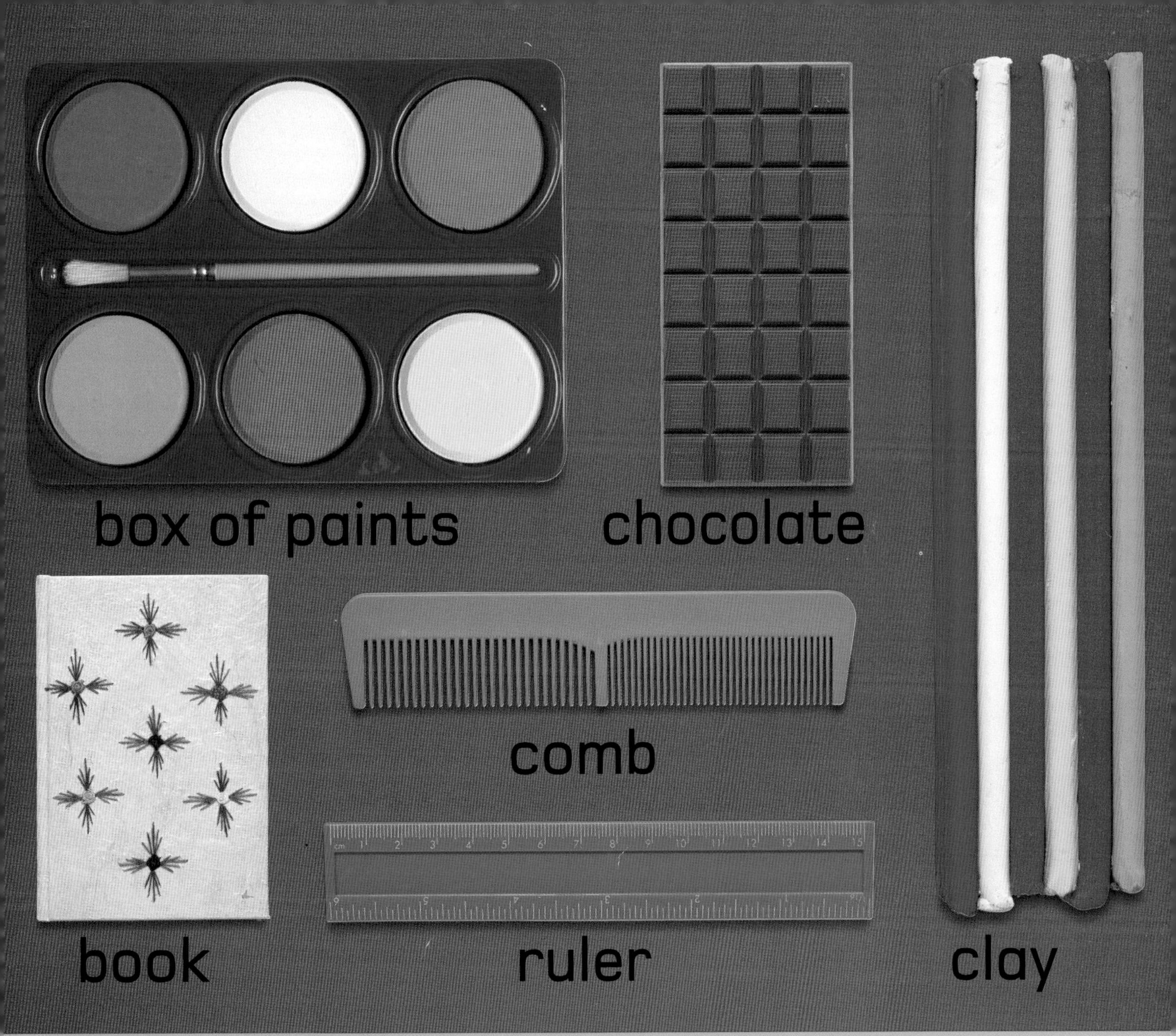

Which paint colors can you see?

Diamonds

candy

badge

wooden tiles

box

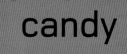

stickers

Can you count the wooden tiles?

earrings

present

kite

What colors are on the kite?

Stars

Can you count the lily's petals?

How many stars can you count?

Ovals

shells

olives

balloon

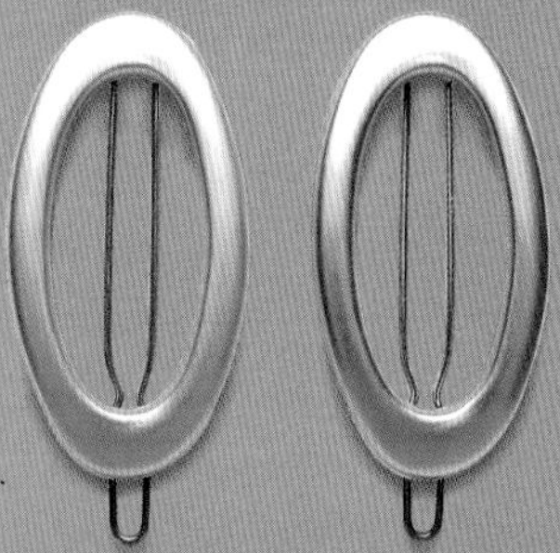

barrettes

mango

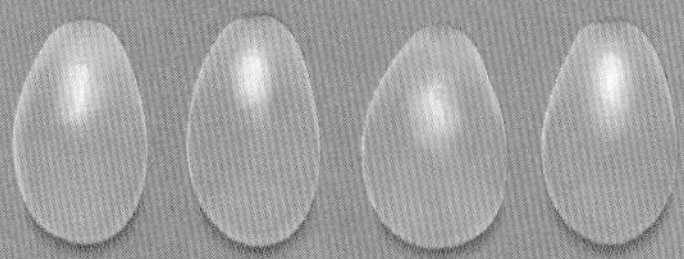

grapes

Can you count the gold things?

picture frame

beans

pebbles

chocolate egg

melon

egg

Can you see some things to eat?

Rings

doughnut

snacks

necklace

hair tie

bagel

tape

Which thing can make music?

colored rings

tambourine

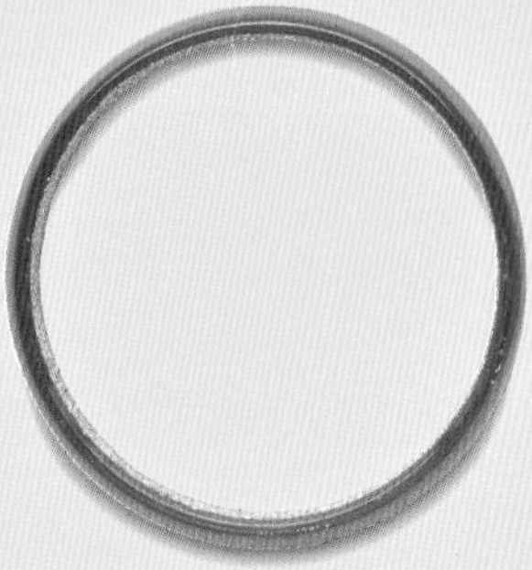

bracelet

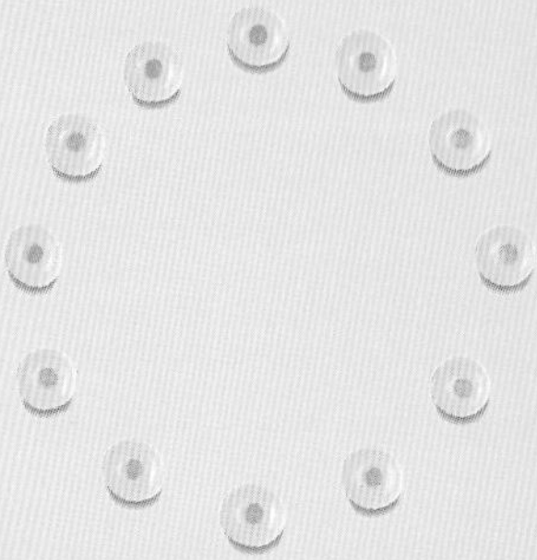

beads

cookies

Can you count the colored rings?

Hearts

candy

stickers

soap

key ring

glitter

trinket box

sunglasses

cookie

chocolate

buttons

handbag

cookie cutter

box

Spirals

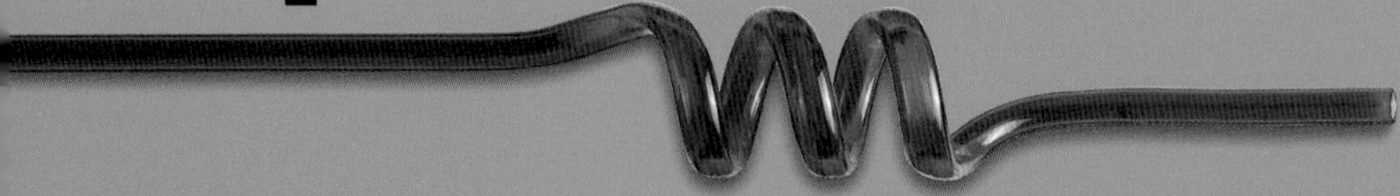

drinking straw

ribbons

spring

shell

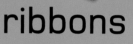

pasta

Do you like to eat pasta?

Zigzags

letters

earrings

snake

toy steps

ribbons

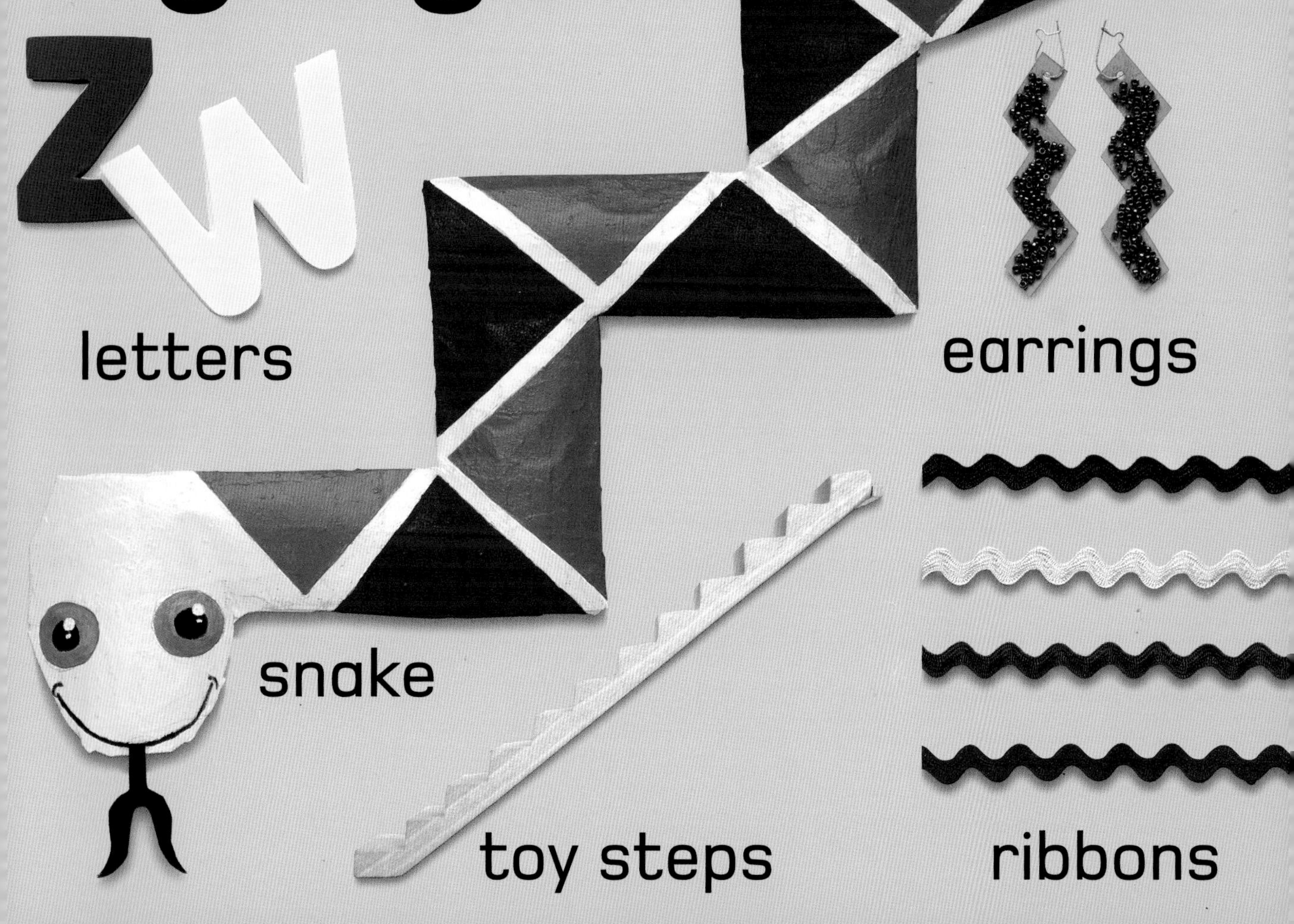

What shape?

doughnut

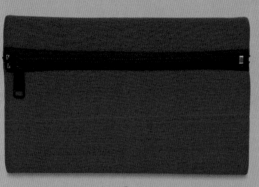

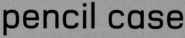

pencil case

chocolate

badge

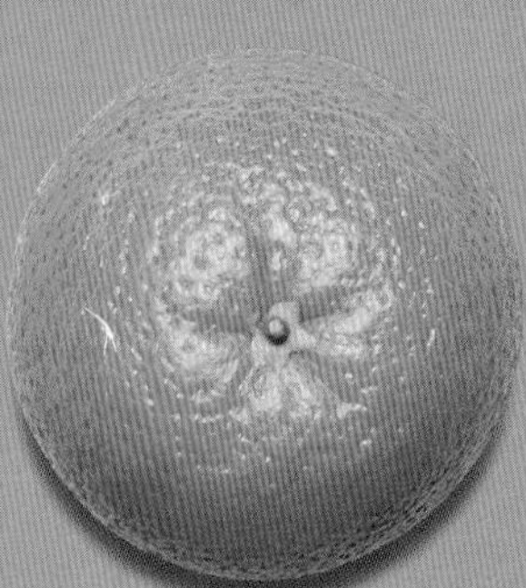

orange

cookie

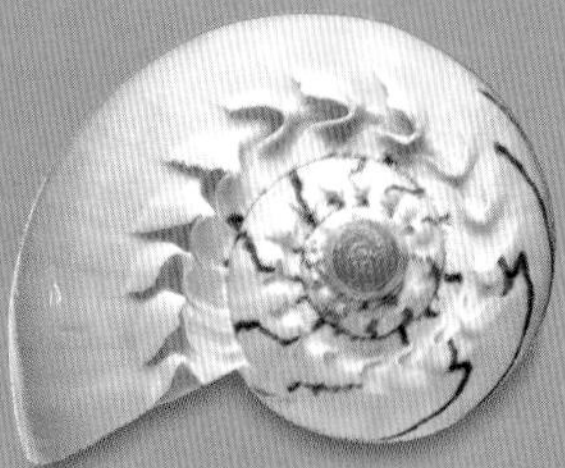

shell

What shapes can you see?